Cat Diaries

Secret Writings of the
MEOW Society

Betsy Byars
Betsy Duffey
Laurie Myers

Illustrated by **Erik Brooks**

SQUARE
FISH

Henry Holt and Company ❖ New York

Special thanks to Amy Myers for her
translation of Chico's story.

SQUARE
FISH

An Imprint of Macmillan
175 Fifth Avenue
New York, NY 10010
mackids.com

Our books may be purchased in bulk for promotional, educational, or business use. Please
contact your local bookseller or the Macmillan Corporate and Premium Sales Department at
(800) 221-7945 ext. 5442 or by e-mail at MacmillanSpecialMarkets@macmillan.com.

Library of Congress Cataloging-in-Publication Data
Byars, Betsy.
Cat diaries : secret writings of the MEOW Society / Betsy Byars, Betsy Duffey,
and Laurie Myers ; illustrated by Erik Brooks. .
p.   cm.
Summary: On one night every year, cats in the MEOW Society, which stands
for "Memories Expressed in Our Writing," gather to read from their diaries, hearing
stories of a gypsy cat, a Caribbean pirate cat, a library cat, and many others.
ISBN 978-1-250-07328-0 (paperback)   ISBN 978-1-42996-375-6 (ebook)
[1. Cats—Fiction. 2. Diaries—Fiction.] I. Duffey, Betsy. II. Myers, Laurie.
III. Brooks, Erik, ill. IV. Title.
PZ7.B9836Cat 2010   [Fic]—dc22   2009018877

Originally published in the United States by Henry Holt and Company, LLC
First Square Fish Edition: 2016
Book designed by Véronique Lefèvre Sweet
Square Fish logo designed by Filomena Tuosto

7   9   10   8

AR: 1.0 / LEXILE: 550L

With esteemed regard
for Sasha Black and Ed Stripe

—E. B.

Contents

CHAPTER 1

Full Moon, Empty Streets

It was the third full moon of the year when cats around the world began to disappear. The alleys and streets were quiet. Trash cans stood untouched, lids strangely in place. Dogs sniffed the air anxiously while mice ran freely, unafraid of predators. Music drifted from apartment windows, unaccompanied by feline howls.

The cat population had a meeting to attend. Large and small, old and young, cats headed to an old abandoned theater. When the room was filled, the eyes of the cats focused toward the front, where

a large gray cat with battle scars made his way to the stage. He spoke.

"I, Ebenezer, call the meeting to order."

"This better be good," called a calico from the back. "I had to plot for three days to get out of the house to come." A Siamese slunk back and forth along the sideline. "And I don't have claws, so I took a big risk getting here."

A fat cat yelled, "It rained yesterday. You know how I hate to get my feet wet, but I did it just to get here, even though I heard we might be meeting with dogs."

"Dogs?" a kitten asked, shaking.

"That was just a rumor," Ebenezer said. "There was some discussion about a possible meeting with the WOOF Society, Words of Our Friends. You see, dogs have written diaries too."

"Dogs? Diaries? Our dog can't even clean himself," a cat yelled.

"How many dogs have enough sense to write a diary?" said an alley cat.

"I agree. The dog in my house could no more write a diary than climb a tree."

"Not so fast," Ebenezer said. "I've read some dog diaries. The stories are not bad."

11

Yowls erupted. Ebenezer waited for the sounds to die down, then spoke. "On to our business."

"Tell us more," called a young cat from the third row. "This is my first meeting."

"As many of you know, for some time now we have been collecting writings by members of our feline community. We call this group MEOW (Memories Expressed in Our Writing)."

Meows of agreement echoed throughout the room. A paw went up.

"Yes, Cisco."

Cisco cleared his throat.

"Hairball," someone yelled from the back. Several cats laughed. Others coughed.

"Order!" called Ebenezer. "Cisco, go ahead."

"What kinds of writings will we hear tonight?"

"There are many different tales."

"Not from the Manx," someone yelled. "They don't have tails."

Everyone laughed, except the Manxes, who hissed.

Ebenezer continued. "Throughout history, cats in their own quiet way have been writing stories—stories of their lives and the lives of others. Tonight, we will hear diaries from a Gypsy cat, a pirate cat, and many more."

"Let's get started," called an Abyssinian.

"We will begin with the diary of a cat named Fuzzy, who learned that it's a delicate balance to keep the best of both worlds. Now, get comfortable."

Some cats curled into balls, others tucked their front paws neatly underneath their bodies. Everyone settled into position and awaited the first reading.

"Fuzzy, please come forward for the reading of the first of the cat diaries."

CHAPTER 2

Fuzzy's Two Worlds

DECEMBER 15

Today my family brought a tree into the house. You heard right, they brought a real tree *in*. This is a special treat for me because I don't go out much. Some cats love *out*. I don't. I love *in*, where it's warm.

When the tree first arrived I sniffed it over and over. I sat underneath the tree while my family hung things on it—fuzzy things, shiny things, round things, things of different shapes and sizes. My favorite is a shiny red ball. It's better than all my cat toys put together.

I plan to sleep under the tree all night and let the rich smell of pine fill my nostrils. Now that I have my own tree, my life is complete. I have the best of both worlds, *in* and *out*.

DECEMBER 16

Today my life is *not* complete. Today I do *not* have the best of both worlds.

This morning I was under the tree letting the smell of pine wash over me, when suddenly I had the most fantastic idea. I decided to *climb* the tree. I have sharp claws. I could do it.

I looked up. My red shiny ball was hanging on one of the top branches, swinging slightly as if to say, "Come on up."

"I'll be right there." I purred.

I tested the tree, first with one paw, then the other. It felt firm, solid. I started up, squeezing past branches, dodging lights. I was halfway up when I stopped to swat at a few items hanging from the outer branches. It was fun!

I continued to climb—past balls, past beads. Then I felt a slight sway. I stopped. It must have been my imagination. I moved slowly to the next branch. Another sway. I paused to give the tree a chance to settle down.

I gazed across the room. The view was fantastic. I could see everything. What a great spot! If I could get a little higher, it would be even better. I could stay there all day, and no one would be able to see me.

I moved carefully to the next branch. Yes indeed, this was perfect.

Wait a minute! Did the tree move again? No. Wait. Yes. It did move. It's moving more. This is not good. Not good at all. I think I'm going doooooooown.

The tree crashed into the middle of the room, taking me with it. We hit the floor with balls and beads flying everywhere. Then it was quiet. I got up and shook myself off. What do you know? The shiny red ball was right at my feet. I batted it around a few times.

"Fuzzy?" someone yelled from another room.

"Fuzzy!" others cried, hurrying in.

I was beginning to get a bad feeling about this. They weren't happy. Someone picked me up.

"Fuzzy. OUT," someone yelled.

"*Out?*" I meowed. "I love *in*. Wait. Don't put me OOOOOOOOOOOOOOOOOUT."

Slam. The door closed. Quickly I ran to the side window. Sometimes they let me *in* when I'm at that window.

"Here I am," I cried, shivering.

They ignored me.

"Let me IIIIIIIIIN," I yelled.

They ignored me. They were busy fixing the tree.

"You know you're going to let me in eventually," I whimpered.

Then I noticed they were hanging my red shiny ball back on the tree, on that same high branch where the good view is. Suddenly, I was not worried.

I'm sure they will let me *in*, because they always do. Soon I will be warm. I will be back under my tree smelling the pine. I will climb to that high branch and sit next to my red shiny ball. Once again I will have the best of both worlds, *in* and *out*.

CHAPTER 3

Rama, the Gypsy Cat

Kansas, 1900
Read by Ebenezer

DAY ONE

"Tonight the music is sad," the Gypsy woman said. I was on her lap, purring.

I have two purrs. Purr-one is a public purr. If anybody does something nice for me, I purr-one.

Purr-two is a private purr. It is deeper, warmer, for one person only. My purr-two is only for the Gypsy woman.

The Gypsy woman hummed and stroked my ears, my golden earring. She put the earring there when I was a kitten. She said, "Now you are a Gypsy like me. We Gypsies keep our eyes to the road ahead."

The Gypsy woman lifted my paw and looked at it. "I'll tell your future, Rama. What will tomorrow bring?"

She didn't like what she saw, for she dropped my paw and sighed.

A sudden breeze brought an interesting smell from the forest. I jumped to the ground.

"No, Rama, no!" she called after me. "Not tonight, Rama! Tonight we—" I never heard the rest.

I caught a mouse first thing, then a fat chipmunk. I saved the chipmunk's foot, a gift for the Gypsy woman.

Rain began to fall. I took shelter in a hollow tree. I was full. I was dry. I slept.

DAY TWO

The rain was harder, slanting into the hollow. I moved deeper inside.

By night I was hungry, but it was still raining. I wanted to be in the Gypsy woman's wagon. I wanted to be on her lap. I wanted to purr-two. I ate the chipmunk foot.

DAY THREE

I left the tree and ran to camp. The clearing was empty. The wagons were gone. The Gypsy woman was gone too.

I saw the wagon tracks and started to follow. I ran like the wind. I was hungry, but I didn't stop to hunt. I was thirsty, but I didn't stop to drink.

The wagon tracks stopped at the river. It was not a deep river. Horses and wagons could cross. Cats could not.

I continued to run, hoping to find a way across. At sundown I smelled smoke. Food was cooking.

I thought it was the Gypsy woman. Maybe she had not crossed the river with the others. She was waiting for me!

I ran to the clearing. I stopped. There was one wagon. It was not the Gypsy woman. A man sat by the wagon. He was singing, but it was not a Gypsy song.

"Too-rah-lie-ooooooh," he sang. The song ended. There was a silence.

I sat in the shelter of the trees and watched.

DAY FOUR

Morning came and still no sign of the Gypsy woman's wagon. The man was sleeping on his blanket. His blanket looked comfortable. I had not planned to, but I meowed. The man looked up and saw me. He beckoned me over. I went slowly. He offered me food. I ate.

Then the man lay back down on his blanket. I sat down too and purred my thanks. The man rubbed my ear like the Gypsy woman did, and he saw my golden earring.

He said, "Me darlin' mother, bless her soul, had such earrings back in Ireland."

I answered, "Meiow."

We began to talk. The man said, "Do you think you'd like to be a peddler's cat? If so, then, me darlin', you're welcome to ride along."

I said, "Meiow."

After a while, he pulled me into the crook of his arm and closed his eyes.

I was full. I was warm. I was content.

The man was content too. A human purr-two rumbled inside his chest. I made a decision. My purr-one became deeper, warmer. Now it was a purr-two. The man and I purred ourselves to sleep together.

DAY FIVE

The peddler's wagon pulled out of the clearing. I sat on the seat beside the man. I glanced over my shoulder to the river and then turned my eyes to the road ahead.

CHAPTER 4

Library Cat

There's a large hedge in front of an old redbrick building at the corner of Irwin and Vine streets. In front of that building I was born and lived, but inside that wonderful building I found my life.

One morning a big yellow bus pulled up in front. Children got off and I watched. I felt small and afraid, but my curiosity got the best of me. When they went up the steps and through the door, I followed. I figured out that building was called the library.

The library was an amazing place, warm and quiet. The children's voices hushed as they filed through the rows of books and settled in a most

wonderful place. It was a room filled with sun, a floor covered with pillows of every color, and walls lined with the most amazing things. Books.

I snuggled down beside a girl who began to stroke my back. I purred softly and felt pure contentment. Sun filtered in through the windows, and the children shifted and found comfortable resting spots. A man in a red sweater with a kind face settled in a rocking chair, picked up a book from the top of the stack, and began to read.

In the story, an old man and his wife gave one lonely kitten a home. But then the old man and woman took in more and more cats until they had millions of cats. Finally the cats disappeared, and the one cat was left.

As I listened to the story my heart pounded. I hung on every word and I learned about myself. I

could be loved too. Maybe I could find a home like the kitten in the story. I rolled over beside the girl and slept. This might be the perfect home.

When the children left, I stayed, snuggling down in the colored pillows.

The man in the red sweater said, "Well. What have we here?" He picked me up and looked me over. I purred and rubbed my head on his hand. He rubbed back. I liked the man right away.

"Okay," he said. "Maybe you can stay . . . but just till we find you a home." He made a sign that said FREE KITTEN. He gave me half of a tuna sandwich and a bowl of water.

That afternoon more children came and I hurried to the story nook. I sat by the man's feet and looked up expectantly. He read a story about an incredible journey. A cat and his companions traveled across the country having adventures. I drew closer to the man's feet. I did not want to go on any adventures. But as I listened, I felt my heart pound harder and

I experienced the adventures too. As I listened to their story I learned about myself. I could be brave, if I needed to. I could have adventures, if I wanted to. I purred. Or maybe not.

That night, alone in the dark library, I was afraid. But I grew brave thinking about the story. I wandered through the great rooms. It was dark, but I could find my way easily through the shelves. I explored the library. I sniffed every corner. From one room there were scratching noises, and I hurried back to the pillows and hid. I wasn't ready for that room yet. I was happy to see the man come the next morning. I rubbed around his leg and purred.

That day more children came, and he read a story about the history of Egypt. During a battle the Egyptian soldiers had cats to protect their bows and arrows. Without cats, the rats would come and eat the strings off the bows. The Syrian army did not have cats, so when they went to get their bows for battle, the bows had no strings and the Egyptians won the war. Cats saved the day.

I learned about history and I learned about myself. Cats like me were smart. I learned that I could be smart. I walked taller that day. With my head up and my tail straight, I led the children to the door and saw them out.

"Bye-bye, Library Cat," one boy called to me, and I stood tall.

As I explored that night, I crouched and leaped boldly through the dark rooms. As I thought of the room with the scratching sounds, I thought about

the cats in Egypt who saved the battle and fought the rats. I listened and heard the scratching again, but this time I went inside. The next morning when the man came in I put the mouse at his feet as a gift.

"Aha," he said. "I guess we need a cat around here after all." He took the sign that said FREE KITTEN and threw it away. I purred with happiness. The bus arrived, and as I snuggled down that day in the reading nook with the children, something was new: I belonged here.

I listened to another story, a delightful one about a girl who went down a rabbit hole. In the story was a Cheshire cat who had a huge smile, and the smile became so big that the cat disappeared and only the smile was left.

As I nodded off, I smiled. When I heard the story about the cat, I learned about myself. I was no longer small and scared and unsure of myself.

In front of the library I was born, but inside that wonderful building I found my life. I was loved like the little kitten, and brave like the cat who took the journey. I was smart like the Egyptian cats, and my smile was so wide and my happiness so big, that I felt just like that Cheshire cat.

CHAPTER 5

Whiskers and the Parachute

South Carolina, 1943
Read by Whiskers, a descendant
of the original Whiskers

"**F**ind the cat! Find the cat!"

Anytime Johnny wanted to find me, I didn't want to be found. This time he had two kids to help him; I didn't have a chance. They found me under the sofa and took me to the basement.

"What are you making, Johnny?" one kid asked.

Johnny said a word I had never heard before. The kids looked impressed, so I knew it was something terrible. The word was *parachute*.

Johnny said, "I saw parachutes in a war movie last week."

"What's a parachute?" one boy asked. He didn't know either.

"It's a piece of cloth like this," Johnny explained, "with strings like this. When you jump out of an airplane the cloth fills with air and you float safely to the ground."

"It's too small for us. Who's going to try it out?"

In the silence that followed, six eyes turned to me.

All too soon I was yanked up onto the table and my body was wound in strips of cloth. I struggled hard, but there were six hands now and it was hopeless. I let out meows of protest so high and strange they didn't even sound like my meows.

They hooked the cloth onto the top of the strips. Then, with shouts of excitement, they ran up the basement stairs.

Johnny carried me up more stairs and then up the attic stairs and out onto the roof. It was just Johnny and me up there and, of course, the parachute. The other two kids were standing outside, looking up at us.

At that moment the mother came out, and was I glad to see her! This is the only person who treats me the way I like to be treated. I meowed my "help me" meow, but it didn't come out right.

The mother said, "What's going on here?"

One of the kids said, "Johnny made a parachute for the cat. It's a real neat parachute. You—"

"Where is this parachute?"

The kids pointed and the mother looked up.

I meowed again, and this time I managed to get out the strongest "help me" of my life.

"Don't—you—dare!" the mother said to Johnny.

Johnny said, "But, Mom, it's perfectly safe. I promise. I—"

"DON'T—YOU—DARE!"

"Look, Mom," Johnny said. "Will you just take a look at it?" He held me up and shook out the parachute.

"DON'T—"

She never got to finish.

For at that moment a breeze came up. I felt my fur ruffle where it wasn't under the bindings to the parachute, and the breeze ruffled not only my fur but the cloth, too. Before I knew what had happened—*whoosh!*—the parachute and I were on our way.

"I didn't mean to. Mom, I promise I—"

But the rest of his words were lost to me as the parachute and I rose over the roof.

We sailed over the trees. Then we floated over the barn. We were flying like birds! I could see everything.

Just as I was beginning to take in the view, we started down. This sinking happened over the pond. Johnny had once sent me "out to sea," as he called it, on this pond, so my fear redoubled.

Then the blessed breeze blew again. We flew over the cornfield, over a couple of cows, and touched down in a small bush.

The mother was the first to arrive. She picked me up. "Oh, kitty-witty! Kitty-witty!" I love it when she calls me that. "Oh, my precious kitty-witty."

As she said these comforting words, she managed to undo my bindings and throw the accursed parachute on the ground. She stepped on it as we headed for the house.

I knew what would happen now. Johnny would be sent to his room. The two kids would be sent home. The mother would find a wonderful treat for me, and after I had eaten, she would hold me on her lap and stroke my fur and scratch my ears, all the while saying things like "You're the best kitty-witty in the world. Yes, you are."

I don't recommend parachute rides, but if you ever have to make one, I hope it ends like this.

CHAPTER 6

To Catch a Thief

Read by Chico
Translated by Amalia

Mi *nombre es Chico.*
My name is Chico.

Soy el gato más pequeño del mundo.
I am the smallest cat in the world.

Soy pequeño. Pero, ¿puedo impedir un crimen?
I am small. But can I stop a crime?

Hay un cotorro que vive en mi casa.
There is a parrot who lives in my house.

Este cotorro solamente puede decir una cosa, "Socorro. Socorro. Policía."

This parrot can only say one thing: "Help. Help. Police."

Lo dijo muchas veces en su juventud, pero nadie lo ha oído desde hace muchos años.

He said it many times in his youth, but no one has heard it in many years.

Todos piensan que se le olvidó cómo hablar.

Everyone thinks he forgot how to speak.

Un día oigo un sonido.

One day I hear a noise.

Soy pequeño. Paso desapercibido al cuarto.

I am small. I slip unnoticed into the room.

Veo a un ladrón robando joyas y dinero.
I see a thief taking jewelry and money.

Corro al cotorro. Él no sabe lo que pasa.
I run to the parrot. He does
not know what is happening.

Hay sólo una cosa que hacer.
There is only one thing to do.

Subo a la jaula.
I climb up to the cage.

*El cotorro encrespa sus plumas. No le gusta que
yo este cerca de su jaula.*
The parrot ruffles his feathers. He does not like
me near his cage.

*Subo a la copita que contiene sus semillas espe-
ciales.*
I climb up to the small cup that holds his special
seeds.

*Estas semillas vienen de Bolivia. A él, las semi-
llas son como joyas, sin precio.*
These seeds come from Bolivia. His seeds are like
priceless jewels to him.

Consigo pasa, mi pata entre los barrotes y robo unas semillas.

I squeeze my paw through the bars and steal some seeds.

Es más de lo que puede aguantar.

This is more than he can stand.

Al final grita, "Socorro. Socorro. Policía."
At last, he cries, "Help. Help. Police."

Pronto, oigo las sirenas.
Soon I hear sirens.

La policía llega.
The police arrive.

El ladrón es capturado.
The thief is caught.

Soy el gato más pequeño del mundo. Pero, ¿puedo impedir un crimen?
I am the smallest cat in the world. But can I stop a crime?

¡Sí!
Yes!

❖ CHAPTER 7 ❖

Miu: The Great Cat of Egypt

Egypt, circa 2000 B.C.
Read by Digger, cat of Sir Henry Boneman

THOU ART THE GREAT CAT, THE AVENGER OF
THE GODS, AND THE JUDGE OF WORDS, AND THE
PRESIDENT OF THE SOVEREIGN CHIEFS AND
THE GOVERNOR OF THE HOLY CIRCLE; THOU
ART INDEED THE GREAT CAT. *(Inscription on
the Royal Tombs at Thebes)*

I am the Great Cat, Miu. To look at me you would
not suspect I am a god. I am small but powerful.
When I walk through the marketplace, the people
bow. My image decorates the temple and is worn
on amulets and earrings. Dreams of the Great Cat

mean a good harvest. Mortals adorn my ears with jewels and gold. They honor me.

There is only one who does not worship me. One who does not bow down in the marketplace. One who drools in the presence of Miu.

It is Abu, the Royal Dog.

I move with the timelessness of the centuries. I scorn mortals who hurry to get here and there. I look down upon the horses and lesser beasts that clomp and run with nervous energy. Chariots stop to allow me to pass. No one gets in my way when I take my regal walk.

There is only one who has the nerve to interrupt my walk. One who comes at me, with yips and barks that make my fur rise. One who makes me lose my composure and even *hisss*!

It is Abu, the Royal Dog.

My fur is perfect, groomed daily, by mortals and by me. A cat, especially the Great Cat, Miu, must be perfect. I lick each paw often to make sure it is free of the dust and dirt from the streets. I keep my whiskers free from drops of milk and honey. I am praised for my cleanliness.

There is only one who does not value the cleanliness of Miu. One who tromps into the palace slinging drool and mud as he shakes his filthy body. One who has the nerve to place a dirt-laden paw on the Great Cat.

It is Abu, the Royal Dog.

The servants bring me offerings, bits of fish and bowls of fresh milk. They place the offerings before me and bow reverently. No one touches the offerings to the Great Cat, Miu. On fear of death no one comes near while the offerings are consumed.

There is only one who dares to interrupt the feast of Miu. Only one irreverent, greedy, clumsy oaf who comes running and sniffing to grab the royal bits of fish and milk.

It is Abu, the Royal Dog.

I maintain my composure at the temple. I stand  motionless and dignified, like a statue. I am surrounded by statues of other cat gods who have come before me. We stand tall. We are pictures of perfect composure. No one bothers the Great Cat, Miu. But, as I hold my pose, I hear yipping outside. One statuesque ear bends forward. I pull it back. I will not be disturbed. I stand taller and make my eyes into small slits. The yapping continues and my perfectly still tail flips unbidden. Again it flips and I cannot stop it. The yipping increases in volume. Involuntarily, the hairs rise on my back.

No one dares to enter the holy space and disturb the calm, no one except . . . In he comes! I jump up and lose my pose. My back arches, fur stands in all directions, and I give out an ungodly growl.

It is Abu, Abu, ABU!!! The Royal Dog!

At night sometimes I prowl. I catch the mice who invade the granary. After a good hunt I walk home. The world is bigger at night and sometimes I feel alone. It is cold in the desert and there are noises. I hurry past the pyramids and sphinx. When I look up at the golden moon hanging in the sky and the twinkling of a million stars, I don't feel so much like the Great Cat. I feel very small and I hurry faster.

Then I reach the marketplace. The moon glows, illuminating strange shapes on the streets, and I hurry even faster. I need a friend. I pause outside the royal kennel. All is quiet.

Up I go through the window, for there is one inside who I know can protect me. One who will keep the shadows away. One who is an irreverent, greedy, clumsy oaf, but one who is my friend in the darkness. I tiptoe across the royal cushions and I snuggle up for warmth and protection. *Purrrrrrr.* I sleep safe and warm against his back.

It is Abu, the Royal Dog.

CHAPTER 8

Go-Go Goes Bananas

My name is Go-Go, and you have probably seen me in a book. *Go-Go Goes to the Farm. Go-Go Goes to the Zoo. Go-Go Goes to Camp.*

Only I don't go to any of these places. I stay home with Arthur. I watch him write the books. I watch him draw the pictures.

He will show me a picture and tell me what a good time I had. "Go-Go, look what fun you had at the ice rink. Look at your double axel!

"Go-Go, look what fun you had at your birthday party. See the cake shaped like a bird. You got candy feathers caught in your teeth."

Only I didn't get to skate or eat feathers. I stayed right here in the studio.

Now, at last, I was going somewhere. My books were so popular that Arthur was invited to a school. I was invited too.

The school had a room filled with children and books. I was the star. I heard my name everywhere. "It's Go-Go! Look, it's Go-Go in person!"

We made our way to a small table covered with Go-Go books. Arthur sat and I made myself comfortable on a stack of books.

The children lined up to get books, and Arthur got right to it. He opened the first book and wrote something inside.

"Go-Go's going to autograph my book too," a girl cried. A teacher got her camera ready.

Then a terrible thing happened. Arthur took my leg, pressed my paw first onto a wet black pad and then onto the book beside what he had written. The children clapped excitedly.

"Mine next," a boy cried out.

Now, I am very, very particular about my paws. I lick them clean even when they are clean, and so my horror at this black, wet paw was unbounded.

I leaped from the table, scattering the books in all directions, and ran. There were cries from the children.

"Catch her."

"Go-Go! Come back!"

I paid no attention.

I ran through the room, scrambling between the many legs of the children in line. Children jumped out of the way.

"There goes Go-Go."

"Chase her."

I hurried into another room where children were eating on trays. I leaped over a table. I flew over or ran around everything in my way. Milk boxes and corn dogs hit the floor. A girl in line jumped back, bumping into the other children. Trays were tipping. Lima beans were flying. A blob of mashed potatoes

49

just missed a teacher. I scurried down the lunch line. The children joined the chase.

On I went, down the hall through a door that said PRINCIPAL. I jumped across a desk covered with papers, leaving a trail of black paw prints. The man at the desk yelled, "Stop!" then jumped up and ran after me with the children.

They chased me down a hall into a huge room filled with chairs and a stage with a curtain. All the chairs were filled with even more children. A woman behind a podium was speaking. She was very serious, and when she saw me, her mouth dropped open in surprise. The children cheered and clapped for me. I looked at the curtain and didn't hesitate. Up I went. At the top I settled on a small ledge and gazed out at the children. They were clapping and cheering. It was nice to hear the children cheering for me.

I looked at my paw. It wasn't as bad as I had thought. A lot of the black had come off in my run. The children were calling, "Go-Go, come down." But I ignored them.

It took a lot of licking to get my paw really clean. When I was satisfied at last, I glanced down. I liked it up here. I liked everyone looking at me. It was like I was a king, and the whole school was my kingdom. Arthur was holding out his arms.

The look on his face told me he had learned something about a cat's paws. I backed down the curtain and fell into his arms. The children applauded.

Someone yelled, "Is your next book going to be *Go-Go Goes to School*?"

Someone else said, "Go-Go looked happy being up so high. His next book should be *Go-Go Goes into Orbit.*"

"How about *Go-Go-Goes to the Moon*?"

Those children ought to be writing my books instead of Arthur.

We went back to the room with the books, and Arthur signed every one. I did not. I sat on a stack of books and let each child pat me.

On the ride home Arthur said, "Actually, I ought to bring you with me more often. You're the star."

That was the nicest compliment he ever paid me. I can't wait to see where we'll go next.

❖ CHAPTER 9 ❖

My Adventures

There's a special place by the window in the living room where the sunshine comes in and warms the floor. That's where you will find me, lying in that rectangle of warmth—dozing, stretching, and being thankful for my home. The sunlight feels good on my fur and reminds me of what it was like to be young.

I haven't been young in a long time. My claws are gone. My teeth are old and dull. My ears miss many sounds. My once sleek body is rounded and soft, and as I roll about in the shaft of light I get sleepy and I dream . . .

◆ ◆ ◆

Suddenly, it is night and I am standing in the moonlight, thinking of the beautiful Tabby next door. But wait! There is another suitor present. Behind the hedge, there is a competitor for her affections.

"MMMRRRROOO!" I recognize his howl. It is my enemy, the one-eared black cat from down the street.

"VAVAVOOOOM!" I hear him call a serenade to Tabby.

I answer with my distinctive howl from deep in my soul. "ROOWWWWW!"

He stops his serenade. For a moment I lose track of him. Where is he? Is he sneaking around to ambush me? I hear a trash can fall next door. He is in Tabby's backyard!

"ROOWWWWW!" I call out a warning to him.

"MMMMRRRRROOOO!" He answers back a challenge. I know where he is.

"ROOWWWW!" I leap over the back fence, and we square off.

"MMMMRRRRROOO!"

"ROOWWWW!"

We circle each other in the night. We growl and howl. We tense our bodies and then . . . I leap! Rolling and clutching we battle for beautiful Tabby. I am winning! I am winning!

My one-eared opponent runs for the hedge and disappears.

"ROOWWWW!"

I am victorious!

❖ ❖ ❖

I yawn and stretch, greatly satisfied with the warm remembrance of my victory. The sunlight patch has shifted a little in the afternoon and I roll over into the new position. *Purrrrr.* The sun is bright and I must close my eyes . . .

* * *

Suddenly, I am younger, stronger. I run swiftly through the neighborhood, past houses and street-lights. The neighborhood gives way to the forest, and the ground becomes wild with bushes towering over me. I am running and leaping and the wind is blowing my whiskers. I am free! But wait! There's a sound in the distance. A yip and a bark signaling danger. I freeze.

The yip grows closer . . . closer. I see him, the bulldog from the end of the cul-de-sac, drawing closer. His big cat-biting mouth is open and drooling, his huge cat-pounding paws are pulling him closer. I stand my ground and watch his charge. I do not blink. Just as he rounds the bend, his teeth snapping with anticipation, I leap. I leap gracefully, hanging in the air for a moment like a cloud, then land with perfection on a branch just out of reach. He snaps and yips and howls with despair. I slowly lick my paws and smile.

The sun on the floor is warm as I stretch my satisfied stretch and extend each paw one by one. My escape was magnificent. I roll gently to the other side and again I close my eyes . . .

Suddenly, I am back in the forest. My predator is gone. I jump nimbly from the branch to the ground and pause to sniff the forest air. I listen with my keen ears to the forest sounds. The wind blows the trees. The water in a nearby brook bubbles. But wait! There is a crackle in the brush over to the right behind the oak tree. A small noise. There it is again. Now a crinkle and a crackle. Only the keenest feline ears would have picked it out. I crouch and wait. My body tenses. I shift from side to side and wait.

Crinkle. Crackle. The noise draws closer. . . .

Crinkle. Crackle. I think it is my old nemesis the chipmunk. Yes! I see him now nosing in the dry leaves. My muscles tighten, but I remain as still as a statue, waiting for the perfect moment. Waiting . . . waiting. . . .

Crinkle. Crackle.

POUNCE!

◆ ◆ ◆

I wake up, startled, but greatly satisfied by my day's activities. The sun is fading now from the floor by the window, and I roll over and with a little difficulty stand up. I blink a few times and smile, remembering my adventures. Then I hear the sound of food dropping into my bowl. Even old ears can make out this pleasant sound. Even old legs can trot toward the kitchen for dinner.

CHAPTER 10

Pirate Cat, Treasure Hunter

The Caribbean, 1717
Read by Tiger

"**Y**o-ho! Yo-ho! A pirate's life for meeeeeeeee."

Yes indeed, mate. The day I set foot on Captain Blackbeard's ship, I knew a pirate's life was for me.

I don't look much like a pirate. I don't wear an eye patch—both my eyes are quite fine. And I don't have a peg leg. But I'm a pirate nonetheless.

It happened by accident. I was on the docks when a big catch arrived. I found a fishtail and I slipped inside a crate to have a little privacy while I finished it off. The crate was loaded onto a ship and I set sail with Blackbeard.

For as long as I've been with them, Blackbeard and his men have searched for the treasure of a man named Hollingsworth. They want it bad. It's hidden on an island somewhere in the Caribbean and we have sailed to and fro looking for that treasure.

One day Blackbeard yelled, "Gather around, men."

It was seldom Blackbeard called us all together, so I was curious. I jumped onto the railing beside him. He stroked my back as he spoke.

"I've new information that the Hollingsworth treasure is at Gorda Island. We set sail immediately."

With that the men erupted in cheers.

The wind was steady and strong and the sails filled to capacity. We cut through the water with graceful speed.

Several hours later the lookout yelled, "There she stands."

I leaped to the railing and got my first look at Gorda Island. *Gorda* means big, and big it was.

"Where do we drop anchor, Captain?" one of the crew asked.

"North by the caves."

We pulled close and set anchor. The men lowered the rowboats into the beautiful blue waters.

"Bring Coral," Blackbeard called.

He named me Coral because I am orange and white like the coral in the sea, except for a small

patch of black fur on my chin and on my tail. I think I look a little like Blackbeard.

"That cat doesn't like rowboats," One Arm said.

"Coral goes where I go."

One Arm was right. I don't like the rowboats. They are small and tippy. I started for the ladder to hide below deck. But, *whoosh*, One Arm grabbed me up.

"I don't like rowboats," I cried.

"Nice kitty," he said.

"I don't like rowboats."

"Nice kitty."

"I said I don't like rooooooooooooo—"

One Arm tossed me into the rowboat. One Arm does not like kitties.

I sat on the seat next to Blackbeard. The breeze was light and the waves mild as could be. The water was a deeper blue than usual. We glided into a sandy piece of land and the men began searching.

When I stepped into the first damp cave, I smelled mice. I headed in search of my own treasure.

"Where's the cat off to?" One Arm asked.

"She's helping us look," the second mate, Crazy Jack, answered.

The men laughed.

I caught a few mice as I wandered through caves, bigger mice than on our ship. From time to time I heard the men's voices. I was sneaking up on one mouse when I noticed a tiny beam of light streaming from a crevice. I squeezed through and entered a cave that shone like the sun on the brightest of days. As my eyes adjusted I realized that the cave was filled with treasure: gold and jewels and more.

I could hear the men in another cave nearby. "There is no treasure here," Blackbeard was saying.

"Back to the ship," One Arm yelled. "We'll search the south side of Gorda."

"Blackbeard, where ye going?" Crazy Jack asked.

"I'm looking for Coral!"

"Time be a-wastin'," Crazy Jack said. "We should find that treasure. We're close. I can feel it."

"We don't leave without Coral," Blackbeard said.

"Your old black heart has a soft spot for kitty," Crazy Jack mumbled.

"Another word from you and I'll tear you apart, you dark-hearted mate," Blackbeard said.

I was glad Blackbeard wanted to find me. I knew he would like this shiny treasure. I leaped onto the back of a tall jewel-studded throne and called loudly, "Meeeeeeow."

"Silence," Blackbeard yelled. "I hear her."

"Meeeeeeow."

"She's up ahead."

"Aaaargh," said Crazy Jack. "Ye're wastin' time."

"Meeeeeeow."

I heard them squeezing through crevices, getting closer.

"Meeeeeeow."

"This way," One Arm yelled.

They squeezed through the final opening and into the gold-filled room.

"Blow me away!" One Arm said.

"Coral found the treasure," Blackbeard said and laughed his big hearty laugh.

Crazy Jack gave me a little bow. "Well now, I be beggin' your pardon, Miss Kitty."

I stood tall and proud on the back of my jewel-studded throne. Blackbeard scratched my neck.

"Load up, gentlemen," Blackbeard said.

The mates were merry at supper that night.

One Arm yelled, "Here's to the treasure of Gorda!"

"To the treasure of Gorda!" the mates shouted.

Blackbeard lifted his glass. "And to Coral who found it."

"Yo-ho! Yo-ho! A pirate's life for meeeeeeeeee."

CHAPTER 11

Georgio's Recipes for Outdoor Cuisine

When I was young I prowled at night with Mama. I ate what she ate. If she ate stale bread from a Dumpster, I did too. If she ate dead raccoon from the road, I did too. Then one night Mama taught me what fine dining was all about, and now I have recipes of my own.

FRESH FISH FILET

Find a nice pond. The water must be still. Lean over and let a small drop of spit fall on the water. At least one fish will be dumb enough to go for it. I always leave the bones for the ants. Ants will eat anything.

ALL-YOU-CAN-EAT EGG BUFFET

If you are lucky enough to see a turtle laying eggs, lie down and wait. When she gets through, uncover the eggs and stuff yourself. Trust me. They won't be nearly as good a week later.

BIRD-TO-GO

Find a bird feeder. Wait in an inconspicuous place. Lazy birds won't go to the trouble of pecking seeds out of the little holes, and will go for those spilled on the ground. You can usually take your pick. Bird-to-Go is strictly a take-out order. If you dine in, the owners of the bird feeder may see you and ruin your perfectly delicious meal.

WHACK-A-MOLEY

Whack a mole before he goes in his hole and you'll have whack-a-moley.

JUNIOR RODENT BURGER

Unless you are very hungry, give rats a pass. Wait for a mouse. Some novice mousers make the mistake of taking the mouse inside, expecting people to praise their hunting skills. Do not do this. People will yell, throw you out, and keep the mouse themselves.

ONE-BITE DELIGHTS (WITH THANKS TO MAMA)

During our prowls one night, Mama and I turned onto a well-lit street. She stiffened. I knew she was on to something. She darted forward. The air was full of flying things.

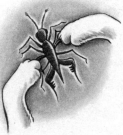

Then Mama did something I'd never seen before. She jumped in the air, grabbed one, and put it in her mouth.

"Go, Georgio!" Mama said after she landed. She was always a cat of few words.

I went. My first jump got me nothing. But I saw one on the ground. I pounced and ate.

The taste was tangy; the body crisp. It was my first cricket. I loved it. As we made our way home I decided to share my fine dining experience with the world.

You may not be lucky enough to catch crickets at midnight, but you may find one in your own backyard. Pounce and eat. When the tangy tartness floods your being, remember to thank Mama and me.

Bon appétit!

CHAPTER 12

Sarge's One Wish

One night in the barn, we played a game called If I Had One Wish.

The cow wished that people would be able to make sense of her moos. This was not my problem. My meows were very expressive.

The horse wished his tail was long enough to brush flies from his face. This was not my problem. No fly would dare to land on my face.

The rooster atop the barn door wished that dawn would hurry up and get here because he was about to burst with cock-a-doodle-dos. This was my problem.

I wanted morning to hurry up so I could get out of this barn and go back in the house, where I belonged.

For years and years I was family. It started when I was a kitten. I was a gift for Major. Major was a boy in bed with casts on his legs. I understood it was up to me to get Major well, and I did.

Major grew up and was gone a lot. I still slept in his bed while he was away. When he came home, he would put his hand on my head and it was just like old times.

Then last week, Major arrived with a woman and a bundle in his arms. Mom and Dad pressed around, making clucking noises. This bundle was the most interesting thing Major had ever brought home.

I could smell milk, and I was beginning to worry that it was a new cat when I got a glimpse. It was a tiny, tiny person. I knew right away it was a new-born. I knew that Major was the father, and the woman that smelled like milk was the mother.

I didn't get a chance to check out the bundle until everyone was at supper. I went into the bedroom and jumped up on the bed. It was a tiny living creature. I was just smelling its breath when Major rushed into the room.

"I thought I heard you," Major said. He didn't seem mad, but the woman behind him yelled, "Bad, bad cat!"

She grabbed me and flung me into Major's arms. "Get that cat out of here."

"It's just Sarge," Major said.

"Out! Either that cat goes or we do."

"I'll handle this," Dad said. He carried me to the kitchen, opened the door, walked to the barn, put me inside, and closed the door.

I'd often been in the barn to chat with the cow or to chase the rooster, but this was different. The door was shut.

Next day Dad came in to milk the cow, but the door stayed shut. I meowed at him and he said, "Sorry, Sarge. I got my orders." I stayed in the barn.

Then one morning, when I had almost given up hope, the barn door opened. It was Major. He put his hand on my head. "You can come out now. We're leaving. Sorry for the inconvenience."

I watched their car disappear, and then Mom held the door open for me. "Welcome home, Sarge."

As I lapped up my milk in the kitchen, I thought about that one-wish game. Maybe there's something to it. Maybe people will make sense of the cow's moos. Maybe the horse's tail will grow longer and the rooster's nights shorter. Or maybe not.

All I know is I got my one wish. I am back in the house, where I belong. I am family again.

CHAPTER 13

Meow! Till Next Year!

The cats were up and meowing with excitement. Some were leaping into the air.

"More diaries," they cried. "More! More!"

Ebenezer held up his paws for silence. "Of course there will be more, but not tonight."

"Awww," the calico cried. "I don't have to be home until morning."

"Me neither," cried another cat.

Ebenezer lifted his paws again. "Order! We have a special guest."

Suddenly a hush fell over the crowd as an old cat stood and made her way to the stage.

"It's Sage," someone whispered.

"*The* Sage? I didn't even know she was still alive."

More whispers were heard.

"She's a legend."

"I heard she was on her fifth life."

"I heard she was on a ship called *Titanic*."

Ebenezer helped her to the podium.

"My good friend Ebenezer, may I say a word to our friends?"

Ebenezer bowed. "It would be an honor."

"Story!" a voice called from the back. "Story!" another requested.

"My dear friends, I'm not here to tell my story tonight, although in a way my story has been told." She gestured to all the cats in the crowd.

ories from our ancestors about wisdom in
ient Egypt, bravery from the pirate cat in the
Caribbean, and adventure from the Gypsy cat are
really stories about all of us."

Meows of agreement arose.

"We've seen ourselves in the dreams and weak-
nesses and humorous looks presented by thoughtful
friends."

More meows of agreement.

"Who hasn't had
encounters with dogs?"—
she paused until the cries of
agreement lessened—"or who
hasn't experienced doubt about
the strangeness of the human world,
like Christmas trees and babies?" Mur-
murs filled the room.

"When we hear the stories of others it reminds
us of our own story. We celebrate our catness in tales
of hunting and adventure and romance."

A few cats coughed in the back, then silence.

"Never forget our motto, MEOW, Memories
Expressed in Our Writing. *Our writing*, my friends,
those are the important words—our writing as
members of MEOW. It is up to us not only to write
our own diaries, but to encourage others to write as

well. You might be surprised to learn there are cats who haven't even heard of a diary. It is up to us to teach them and to become better writers ourselves. I don't think I am being overly optimistic here when I say, not only can we become better writers, we can become the best writers in the history of the world."

There was a rustle of pride and agreement.

"And may I say one more thing, Ebenezer?"

"Yes," the audience cried, not waiting for Ebenezer.

"As I sat here this evening I had a vision. A year from now you will be back. You will bring more diaries and friends with diaries. And there will be cats from all over the world. But most of all, there will be stories, wonderful stories. If I had one wish like Sarge, it would be that I will be here with you to hear them. Thank you."

As Sage left the podium there was a stillness in the room. Then, from the back, from one lone kitten came the sound of a contented rumble, a purr. The rumble grew as the cats settled into a peaceful satisfaction. The rumble carried out into the night air. The alleys and streets once quiet were filled with the sound of contentment. Dogs stopped in their places, ears cocked, puzzled by the sound. Mice looked up in fear and scurried for cover, unsure of the strangeness of the sound.

When the purring died down and Sage was gone, Ebenezer turned to the crowd. "That is an appropriate ending to our meeting. We will adjourn with the reciting of our motto. And this time we will recite it with new meaning. All together now."

"MEOW! MEOW! MEOW!"

The cats looked at one another with new understanding and commitment.

Some cats left, others gathered in small groups to discuss the diaries. On through the night, stories were told, diaries were planned, and at last goodbyes were said. As the cats disappeared into the night their tails were high. Their pride swelled. They were going to be the best writers in the world.

You've heard from Miu, the Great Cat of Egypt—now meet Abu, Miu's canine rival. Find out how Jip leads his master home from the Civil War. Prepare to be dazzled by Tidbit, a star at the Grand Ole Opry.

It turns out cats aren't the only ones with a secret society. . . .

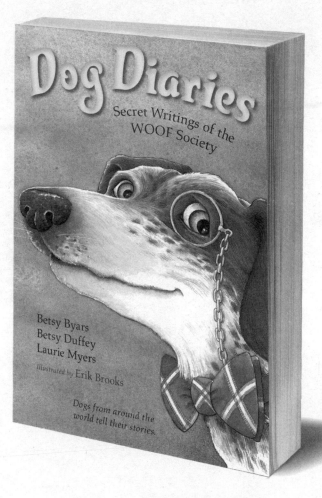

Read on for an excerpt.

CHAPTER 1

Beauregard Presides

In a dark abandoned building, under a rickety staircase, was an entrance, more like a crack between two boards. Light shone behind the boards, beckoning to those outside. Through this mysterious entrance came dogs—large Dobermans, small Pekingese, Scotties, and Pugs. Purebred dogs and dogs of unknown pedigree. Dogs with collars and licenses, and dogs with none.

Inside, the room was surprisingly warm and cozy. The dogs took their places facing the front, where a small podium stood ready. The room was

filled with sound, excited yips and barks, but became silent as an old dog moved toward the podium. His hair was graying at the beard, and his walk had lost the spring of youth, but his eyes shone bright. In his mouth he held a manuscript. He looked out at the group, carefully placed the papers at his feet, and began to speak.

"Welcome, canine friends. Welcome to the meeting of the WOOF Society—Words of Our

Friends. I, Beauregard, your president, am proud to see such a large gathering for this groundbreaking meeting. Let's repeat our motto. All together now!"

The dogs began to chant their motto, each in a different voice.

"WOOF! WOOF! WOOF!"

Beauregard closed his eyes in satisfaction, then examined the crowd.

"As you can see, we have a packed house tonight, so if some of the Chihuahuas wouldn't mind sharing seats, then we'll get started. We all know why we're here, so I won't waste time. Oh, I see a paw raised in the second row. Yes, Pap, you have a question."

An old hound dog blinked. "Why are we here? I forgot. I'm fifteen years old, but remember, that's a hundred and five in people years."

"Yes, Pap, good question. I'll start at the beginning. As you know, for years we have been working to promote a worldwide understanding that dogs have vocabularies beyond *sit, stay,* and *fetch,* that we are indeed accomplished storytellers. Through the dedicated efforts of our membership, we have been collecting stories from dogs across the world and throughout history. Tonight we will be hearing some of those stories."

"Mr. President?"

"Yes, a question from the Newfoundland in the back."

"Will there be any rescue stories?"

"Of course. Daring canine heroes have rescued countless masters from the perils of avalanche and fire. And courageous companions have accompanied their owners into battles and across continents in exploration. There will be a variety of stories, rescue and other-wise."

"What about history?" said a Basset Hound. "I love history."

"Yes, Professor Basset. All through the ages, dogs have faced challenges and had stories to tell. From ancient Egypt to Pompeii to the days of early America. . . . The poodle in the back."

"Well, I hope it's not all history. Today we face new challenges, like bark collars, electric fences—and what about powder-resistant fleas?"

At the mention of fleas, fierce scratching broke out among the members. A small black puppy rolled on his back and wiggled.

"Order, friends," Beauregard said sternly. "We will cover some contemporary issues. Question from the Shih Tzu."

"I hope it's not going to be all stories from big dogs."

"No, there will be stories from many divisions of our canine kingdom, big and small, past and present, smart and . . . well . . . let's just say there will be something for everyone. Question from the small mixed-breed in the second row."

"Who goes first?"

"We will begin with a manuscript from Egypt. Jack's master is an archaeologist, and while his master was digging, Jack did some digging of his own. This was found near a stela from the Eleventh Dynasty. It tells the story of the reign of Intef.

But on the back, unnoticed by humans, is another story, the story of one of our ancestors named Abu, who was the ruler of Egypt.

Excited yips and howls broke out.

"Order! Order! Come to order. The presenters will come forward onc at a time and read their stories."

The dogs leaned forward expectantly as a scholarly-looking Jack Russell Terrier came forward, carrying a small piece of butcher paper.

"Now, without further ado, the WOOF Society presents what we have come to call *Dog Diaries*."

CHAPTER 2

Abu: The Dog Who Ruled Egypt

Egypt, circa 2000 B.C.
Read by Jack

I am the ruler of Egypt.

This is how I know that I am the ruler of Egypt: When I bark, the royal cook rushes to fill up my bowl. He is my servant. When I stand by the door, the royal door opener opens the door for me. He too is my servant. When I stand beside my human, Intef, at the royal throne, people come and bow down. They all serve me! I must be the Pharaoh! All bow before Abu!

My human brushes my sleek hair. His son massages my back and rubs behind my ears. A-h-h! They call me Abu. They too are my servants.

I am great! I am powerful! I am totally in charge! All serve me! Except . . . there is only one who does not serve me. One who does not bow down and serve Abu. One who is disobedient to me. It is Miu, the Royal Cat.

When my human rides in the royal chariot, I lead the way, running fast and moving sleekly. I call out, "Look at me! Look at me! Make way for Abu!"

I lead them past the pyramids and past the giant Sphinx. I lead them into battle, fearless of the arrows and spears that fall around me. I hunt the giant ostrich and keep pace with him step by step. No man or beast can run faster than Abu. I keep pace with the mighty hart as we hunt. I keep pace with the hare. I am the fastest in the world! No beast can escape me. Except . . . there is only one who can escape me. Only one who can race away, jumping to heights that I cannot attain. It is Miu, the Royal Cat.

I have learned to always be in control, to sit with my human at the royal throne, head up and back straight. I have learned to lead the chariots, running straight as an arrow, not looking left or right. I have learned to wait by the door, standing calm and regal. Abu is always totally in control. Always calm and cool and still as the Sphinx. Nothing can make me lose my control. Except...

only one thing can make me lose my control. One creature who can turn me into a scrambling, drooling, running, barking fool. My hair rises unbidden on my back. My lips curl into an unkindly snarl. My front teeth bare. It is Miu, the Royal Cat.

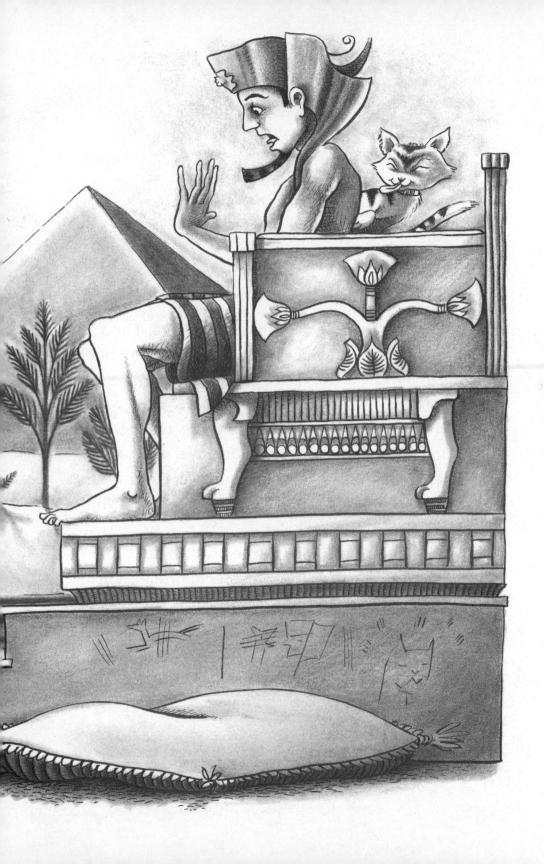

No one touches Abu's royal food bowl. The servants prepare the best for me—roasted tender meat. No one comes near, my bowl is only for the royal Abu. Except one. My water is pure water carried from the royal well. No one touches my water. No one dares to defile the royal water bowl. Except one. And no one dares to sit on Abu's cushion under the throne. Except one—Miu. Miu! MIU, the Royal Cat!

At night I, Abu, sleep in the royal kennel. There are embroidered pillows and comfortable cushions just for my comfort. But . . . it is dark in the royal kennel and a little cold. Sometimes when I am in the kennel and it is cold and dark, I don't feel so much like the ruler of Egypt. I try to be brave. I call out, "I am the Pharoah! I am brave! I am not afraid." My human sleeps in the royal chambers in the palace, his son in the nursery.

The servants and guards have their own places. The royal kennel is a wonderful place, a worthy place for Abu. But . . .

Sometimes when I am lonely, I curl up and close my eyes and long for the morning to come. Sometimes when I am lonely at night, I sleep and hope to dream happy dreams. Sometimes I feel like there is no hope that morning will come. I am all alone. Except . . .

I feel something warm snuggle against my back, and I don't move. I listen to soft breathing and then a low purr. It is Miu, the Royal Cat. And with the comfort of the warmth on my back, I fall asleep.